FORT WORTH PUBLIC LIBRARY

P9-BZI-788

ALADDIN

An imprint of Simon & Schuster Children's Publishing Division

1230 Avenue of the Americas, New York, NY 10020

First Aladdin hardcover edition April 2016

Copyright © 2016 by Frank Asch

All rights reserved, including the right of reproduction in whole or in part in any form.

ALADDIN is a trademark of Simon & Schuster, Inc., and related logo is a

registered trademark of Simon & Schuster, Inc.

For information about special discounts for bulk purchases, please contact

Simon & Schuster Special Sales at 1-866-506-1949 or business@simonandschuster.com.

The Simon & Schuster Speakers Bureau can bring authors to your live event.

For more information or to book an event contact the Simon & Schuster Speakers Bureau at

1-866-248-3049 or visit our website at www.simonspeakers.com.

Designed by Karina Granda

The text of this book was set in Olympian LT Std.

The illustrations for this book were rendered digitally.

Manufactured in China 0216 SCP

2 4 6 8 10 9 7 5 3 1

Library of Congress Control Number 2015944264

ISBN 978-1-4424-6678-4 (hc)

ISBN 978-1-4424-6680-7 (eBook)

In memory and appreciation
of Hugh Lofting

It was a sunny morning and Miss Perkins was in a
sunny mood.

   After feeding her pets . . .

she hopped on her scooter and . . .

drove to her job at the Lending Zoo.

When she arrived, a little late as usual, a line had already formed at her checkout desk.

Everyone in the line had chosen an animal to
borrow from the Lending Zoo.

The last person in line was a young girl Miss Perkins had never met before.

"Hi. My name is Molly," said the young girl. "And I'd like to take home a . . ."

Just then, Mr. Woozel, the Lending Zoo zookeeper, came running down the hall.

"Miss Perkins!" he cried. "Something's wrong with our tiger, Pancake! He refuses to eat his breakfast!"

"I hope he's not ill," said Miss Perkins.

"Shall I call the doctor?" asked Mr. Woozel.

"Not yet," replied Miss Perkins. "Let's go have a look at Pancake first."

"Can I come along?" asked Molly.

"Sure," said Miss Perkins. "Just follow me!"

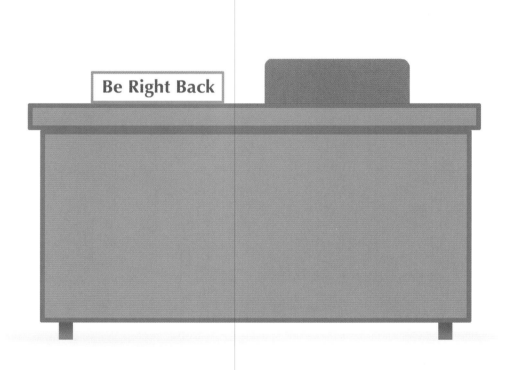

When Miss Perkins, Molly, and Mr. Woozel arrived at Pancake's shelf, they were met with a disturbing surprise.

Pancake was nowhere in sight!

"Oh my!" cried Mr. Woozel. "Pancake must have wandered off. I do hope he's all right."

"Look! Over there!" cried Molly. "Aren't those tiger paw prints?"

"They sure are," said Miss Perkins. "Pancake must have taken a swim in the duck pond!"

"And here's where he left the Lending Zoo," said Molly.

"You're right!" said Miss Perkins.

Then she turned to Mr. Woozel and asked, "Mr. Woozel, would you please keep an eye on my desk while Molly and I go looking for Pancake?"

Miss Perkins and Molly followed Pancake's paw prints down crowded streets . . .

busy beaches . . .

winding lanes . . .

and city rooftops . . .

all the way back to the Lending Zoo!

PANCAKE
The Tiger

"Look! Pancake is back on his shelf," cried Molly.

"Welcome back!" said Miss Perkins as she gave the wayward tiger a great big hug.

Then she turned to Mr. Woozel and asked, "Why don't you try feeding him now?"

When Mr. Woozel offered Pancake his breakfast, the tiger gobbled it up in one bite.

"Pancake seems fine now!" exclaimed Mr. Woozel.

"I guess he just needed some fresh air and exercise!"

"Now tell me," Miss Perkins asked Molly. "What animal did you want to borrow from the Lending Zoo?"

"Actually, I was hoping to borrow a tiger," replied Molly.

"Excellent choice," Miss Perkins said as she issued Molly a Lending Zoo card.

"Have Pancake back by the tenth of May, or you'll have to pay a fine for each day he's overdue."

By then the line at the checkout desk was quite long.
"Now, how may I help you?" Miss Perkins asked a
little boy with a panda in his arms.